Twinkle, Twinkle, Little Star

Retold by MEGAN BORGERT-SPANIOL

Illustrated by SHELAGH MCNICHOLAS with DAN CRISP

CANTATA
LEARNING
MANKATO, MINNESOTA

CANTATA
LEARNING
MANKATO, MINNESOTA

Published by Cantata Learning
1710 Roe Crest Drive
North Mankato, MN 56003
www.cantatalearning.com

Library of Congress Control Number: 2014938325
ISBN: 978-1-63290-066-1 (hardcover)
ISBN: 978-1-63290-355-6 (paperback)

Twinkle, Twinkle, Little Star retold by Megan Borgert-Spaniol
Illustrated by Shelagh McNicholas with Dan Crisp

Book design by Tim Palin Creative
Music produced by Wes Schuck
Audio recorded, mixed, and mastered at Two Fish Studios, Mankato, MN

Printed in the United States of America.

VISIT
WWW.CANTATALEARNING.COM/ACCESS-OUR-MUSIC

On a clear night, we can count thousands of stars. But there are even more that we cannot see. Some stars are bright, and some are **dim**. Some appear to **twinkle**!

When you hear the chime, turn the page.

Twinkle, twinkle little star,
How I wonder what you are.

Up above the world so high,
Like a **diamond** in the sky.

Twinkle, twinkle little star,
How I wonder what you are.

Twinkle, twinkle little star,
How I wonder what you are.

Up above the world so high,
Like a diamond in the sky.

Twinkle, twinkle little star,
How I wonder what you are.

Twinkle, twinkle little star.

How I wonder what you are.

GLOSSARY

diamond—a clear stone that appears to sparkle in the light

dim—not bright

twinkle—to shine or sparkle

Twinkle, Twinkle, Little Star

Public Domain

Traditional

Online music access and CDs available at **www.cantatalearning.com**

TO LEARN MORE

Asch, Frank. *The Sun is my Favorite Star*. San Diego, CA: Harcourt Brace, 2000.

Guillain, Charlotte. *Exploring Space*. Chicago: Heinemann Library, 2009.

Hunter, Nick. *Stars and Constellations*. Chicago: Capstone Heinemann Library, 2014.

Rockwell, Anne F. *Our Stars*. San Diego, CA: Silver Whistle/Harcourt Brace & Co., 1999.

Rustad, Martha E. H. *The Stars*. Mankato, MN: Capstone Press, 2009.